10 TURKEYS
IN THE ROAD

BY Brenda Reeves Sturgis

ILLUSTRATED BY David Slonim

Marshall Cavendish Children

Marshall Cavendish Corporation
99 White Plains Road
Tarrytown, NY 10591
www.marshallcavendish.us/kids

Library of Congress Cataloging-in-Publication Data
Reeves Sturgis, Brenda.
10 turkeys in the road / by Brenda Reeves Sturgis ; illustrated by David
Slonim.— 1st ed.
p. cm.
Summary: Ten turkeys performing circus acts block a country road, much to
the frustration of an angry farmer in a pick-up truck who tries to shoo them away.
ISBN 978-0-7614-5 847-0 (hardcover)   ISBN 978-0-7614-6009-1 (ebook)
[1. Stories in rhyme. 2. Turkeys—Fiction. 3. Circus—Fiction. 4. Counting.
5. Humorous stories.] I. Slonim, David, ill. II. Title. III. Title: Ten turkeys in the road.
PZ8.3.S9229Aai 2011
[E]—dc22
2010001232

The illustrations were rendered in acrylic.
Book design by Anahid Hamparian
Editor: Robin Benjamin

Printed in China (E)
First edition
10 9 8 7 6 5 4 3 2 1

Marshall Cavendish
Children

To all the turkeys in my life: Gary, Stacie, Seabren, Whitney, Seabren IV,
Stephen and Courtney, Stephanie and Shaun, and the newest turkey babies.
We have the greatest show on Earth! To Margery Cuyler and Robin Benjamin,
the best ringmasters in this circus, and to Josh and Tracey Adams—thank
you (no clowning around) for your hard work and friendship! Thank you also
to my good friend Shari Dash Greenspan for everything!

—B.R.S.

To the Stellas,
who gave me my first unicycle

—D.S.

Ten turkeys blocked the road
one hot and hazy day.
A pickup screeched. A farmer beeped.
One turkey flew away.

Nine turkeys in the road
caused a long delay.
The farmer frowned and flashed his lights.
One turkey flew away.

Eight turkeys in the road,
each holding out a tray.
The farmer inched his truck ahead.
One turkey flew away.

Seven turkeys in the road
with cans of string to spray.
The farmer shook his fist and yelled.
One turkey flew away.

SIX turkeys in the road
climbed high to swing and sway.
The farmer banged and clanged his tools.
One turkey flew away.

Five turkeys in the road
declared, "We're here to stay!"
The farmer threw his old straw hat.
One turkey flew away.

Four turkeys in the road
shared a big bouquet.
The farmer opened up his door.
One turkey flew away.

Three turkeys in the road
juggled bales of hay.
The farmer jumped and pulled his hair.
One turkey flew away.

TWO turkeys in the road
squawked, "Hip, hip, hooray!"
The farmer pounded on his hood.
One turkey flew away.

ONE turkey in the road
announced, "We've got to go!"

The turkeys snuck into the truck
and called, "Come see the show!"

One farmer in the road
hung his head and sighed.
A car drove up. The driver asked . . .
"Hey, pal, ya need a ride?"

The tired farmer huffed and puffed,
then squeezed into the car.
The driver squealed, "Away we go!
The circus isn't far!"